HEAD, BODY, LEGS

A Story from Liberia

RETOLD BY

Won-Ldy Paye & Margaret H. Lippert

ILLUSTRATED BY Julie Paschkis

SQUARE FISH ❖ HENRY HOLT AND COMPANY ❖ NEW YORK

About the Story

Head, Body, Legs is a traditional creation story from the Dan people of northeastern Liberia in Africa. Dan mothers and grandmothers tell it to children to illustrate the importance of cooperation—each part of the body is necessary and helps the others, just as each person in a family or a community is necessary and helps the others.

SQUARE FISH

An Imprint of Macmillan

Library of Congress Cataloging-in-Publication Data
Paye, Won-Ldy.
Head, body, legs: a story from Liberia / retold by Won-Ldy Paye and Margaret H. Lippert ; illustrated by Julie Paschkis.
Summary: In this tale from the Dan people of Liberia, Head, Arms, Body, and Legs
learn that they do better when they work together.
ISBN 978-0-8050-7890-9
[1. Dan (African people)—Folklore. 2. Folklore—Liberia.]
I. Lippert, Margaret H. II. Paschkis, Julie, ill. III. Title.
PZ8.1.P24 He 2001   398.2   [E]—dc21   00-44856

Originally published in the United States by Henry Holt and Company
First Square Fish Edition: September 2012
Square Fish logo designed by Filomena Tuosto
The artist used Winsor & Newton gouaches to create the illustrations for this book.
mackids.com

9 10 8

AR: 2.3 / LEXILE: AD220L

For my nieces and nephews in Liberia and in the United States —W. P.

For Alan, Jocelyn, and Dawn
—M. H. L.

To Sam and Seiji
—J. P.

LONG AGO, Head was all by himself.

He had no legs, no arms, no body. He rolled everywhere. All he could eat were things on the ground that he could reach with his tongue.

At night he rolled under a cherry tree. He fell asleep and dreamed of sweet cherries.

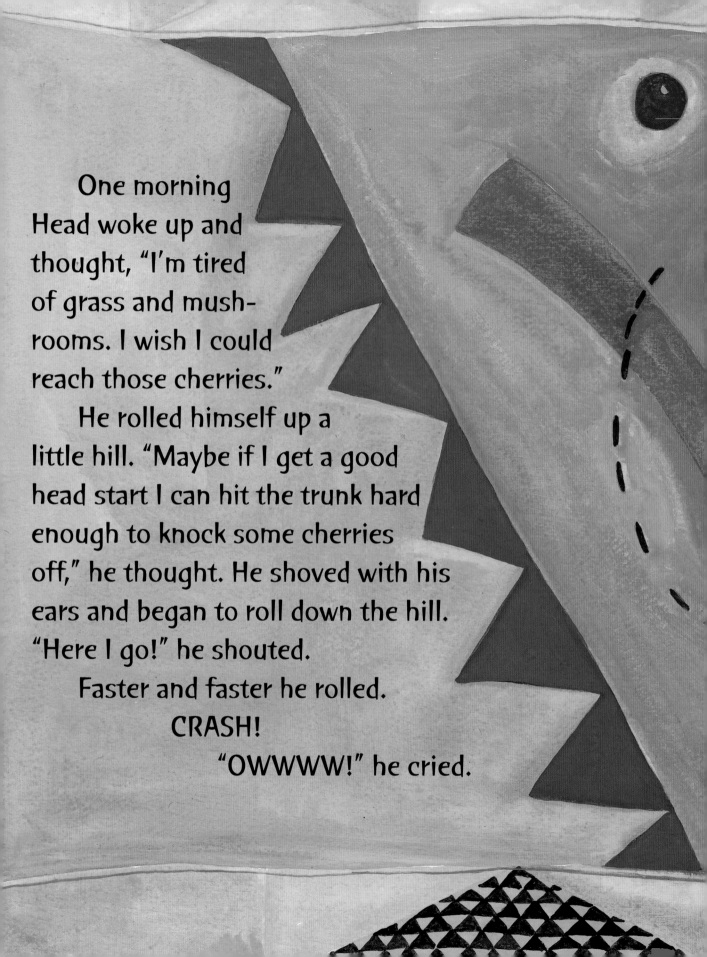

One morning Head woke up and thought, "I'm tired of grass and mush-rooms. I wish I could reach those cherries."

He rolled himself up a little hill. "Maybe if I get a good head start I can hit the trunk hard enough to knock some cherries off," he thought. He shoved with his ears and began to roll down the hill. "Here I go!" he shouted.

Faster and faster he rolled.

CRASH!

"OWWWW!" he cried.

"Who's there?" someone asked.

Head looked up. Above him swung two Arms he had never seen before.

"Look down here," Head said, "and you'll see."

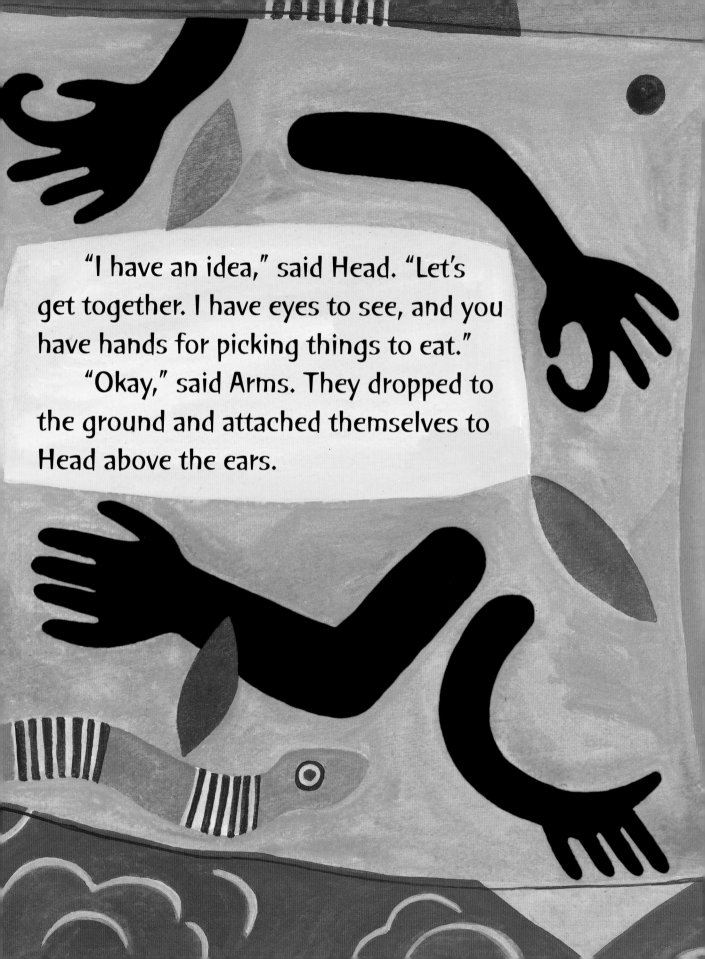

"I have an idea," said Head. "Let's get together. I have eyes to see, and you have hands for picking things to eat."

"Okay," said Arms. They dropped to the ground and attached themselves to Head above the ears.

"This," said Head, "is perfect."

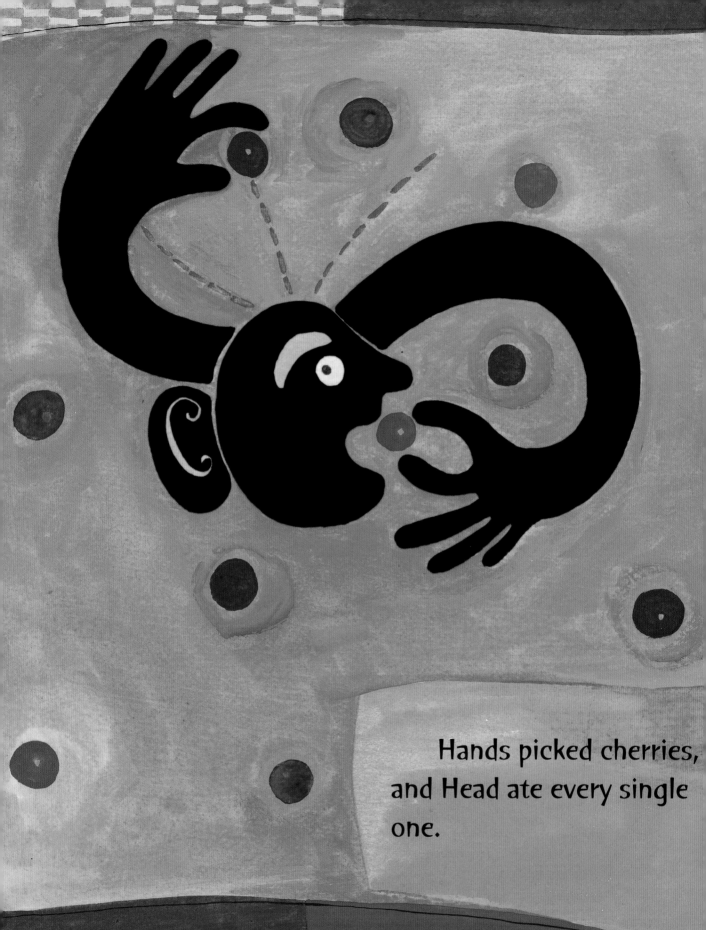

Hands picked cherries, and Head ate every single one.

"It's time for a nap," said Head, yawning. Soon he was fast asleep.

While Head slept, Body bounced along and landed on top of him.

"Help!" gasped Head. "I can't breathe!" Arms pushed Body off.

"Hey," said Body. "Stop pushing me. Who are you?"

"It's us, Head and Arms," said Head. "You almost squashed us. Watch where you're going!"

"How can I?" asked Body. "I can't see."

"Why don't you join us?" said Head. "I see some ripe mangoes across the river. If you help us swim over there, I'll help you see where you're going."

"Okay," said Body. So Head attached himself to Body at the belly button.

"This," said
Head, "is perfect."

They bounced down the bank into the river. "Pull right . . . pull left," Head shouted to Arms, who paddled frantically against the current.

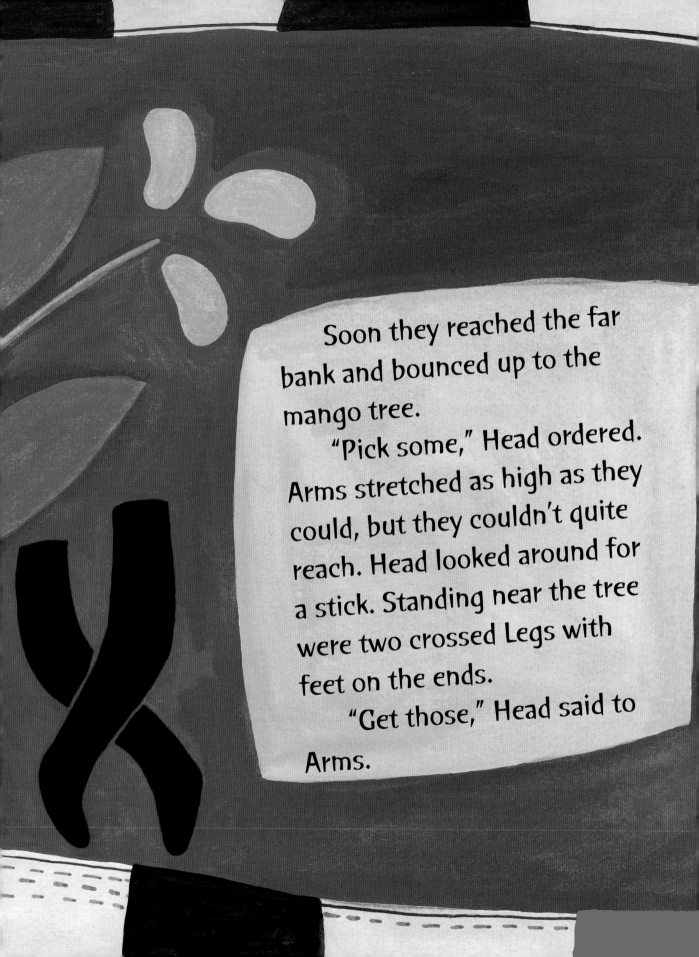

Soon they reached the far bank and bounced up to the mango tree.

"Pick some," Head ordered. Arms stretched as high as they could, but they couldn't quite reach. Head looked around for a stick. Standing near the tree were two crossed Legs with feet on the ends.

"Get those," Head said to Arms.

Arms grabbed them. "Let us go!" shouted Legs.

"Who are you?" asked Head.
"We're Legs. We were
walking but we bumped into
this tree."

"Join us," said Head. "I have eyes. I can show you where to go, and you can help us reach those mangoes."

"Okay," said Legs. So Legs attached themselves to the hands.

"That's right," said Head. "You should be at the bottom, Legs. I'll swing around on top of Body so I can see everything. And Arms, you move to the shoulders."

Everyone slid into place. Legs stood on tiptoe. Body straightened out. Arms stretched up, and the hands picked a mango. Head took a bite.

"Mmm, delicious," Head said.
"Now THIS is perfect!"

An ALA Notable Book for Children

An Aesop Accolade Book for Children

A Bulletin Blue Ribbon Winner

PQY524623

"Delightful."
—The New York Times Book Review

"This will hit story-hour crowds right in the funny bone."
—Booklist

"A very funny story."
—Bulletin of the Center for Children's Books, recommended

SQUARE FISH
AN IMPRINT OF MACMILLAN
175 FIFTH AVENUE, NEW YORK, NY 10010
MACKIDS.COM
PRINTED IN CHINA

$7.99 US / $8.99 Can

ISBN 978-0-8050-7890-9

50799 >

9 780805 078909